Up and Down the River

Also by Rebecca Caudill

Happy Little Family
Schoolhouse in the Woods
Schoolroom in the Parlor
Barrie and Daughter
Tree of Freedom (Newbery Honor)
Saturday Cousins
House of the Fifers
Susan Cornish
Time for Lissa
Higgins and the Great Big Scare
The Best-Loved Doll
The Far-Off Land
A Pocketful of Cricket (Caldecott Honor)
A Certain Small Shepherd
Did You Carry the Flag Today, Charley?
Contrary Jenkins (with husband, James Ayars)
Somebody Go and Bang a Drum

UP AND DOWN THE RIVER

by
REBECCA CAUDILL

Pictures by Decie Merwin

BETHLEHEM BOOKS • IGNATIUS PRESS
Bathgate, N.D.   San Francisco

First Bethlehem Books printing December 2004

ISBN 1-883937-81-7
Library of Congress Card Number 2004113375

Bethlehem Books • Ignatius Press
10194 Garfield Street South
Bathgate, North Dakota 58216
800 757 6831
www.bethlehembooks.com

For

Stella, Will, Cappie, and Clara

through whose childhood

flowed the river

The stories in this book appeared in condensed form in *Jack and Jill*, published by the Curtis Publishing Company.

Contents

1. The Peddler

I do wish we could find some way to get rich, like Althy!" said Bonnie.

Bonnie was talking half to herself, half to Debby. She was stretched on the grass under an apple tree, looking at the advertisements on the back pages of Mother's magazine. Debby was sitting near her, making a pink clover chain to wear around her neck.

Out in the orchard bees buzzed and stopped for business on each big bushy, swaying head of clover.

It was late May, and the sun was warm, and the sweet smell of the blossoms clung to the air.

From the house came the sound of the organ. Sometimes the notes flowed along smoothly like the pebbly stream that skirted the orchard. That was Althy playing. Sometimes the notes balked like a stubborn donkey. That was Clarissy Huff taking a lesson from Althy.

"Althy'll surely be rich before summer's over," said Debby, tying another clover head to her chain. "She gets ten cents for every organ lesson she gives. And she's going to give nine every week."

"How much does that make?" asked Bonnie, who was six and didn't know her multiplication tables yet.

"Ninety cents," said Debby, who was eight and knew her tables straight through twelve times twelve.

"And Emmy's chickens will be hatching out any day now," said Bonnie. "Two hens setting on fifteen eggs apiece—if Emmy sells the chickens for fifty cents apiece, how rich will she be, Debby?"

That was too much arithmetic for Debby to do without a slate and pencil. She answered instead,

2

"You don't count your chickens before they're hatched, Bonnie."

"And Chris will get rich selling ginseng," said Bonnie. "The magazine said, 'Get rich selling ginseng.' He found a little bit in the woods yesterday."

Debby tied another clover head to her chain.

"Can't you find any advertisement in the magazine that tells us how to make money, Bonnie?" she asked.

"Here's something free," said Bonnie. Although she couldn't read words off quickly the way Debby could, she knew the word "free."

Carefully Debby laid aside her clover chain, stretched out beside Bonnie on the grass, and studied the free offer.

The advertisement pictured the State of Ohio, freckled all over with dots as if everybody from Ashtabula to Cincinnati had suddenly broken out with the measles.

" 'Grand Contest! Big Prizes Free! Two Pianos! Cash! Organs! Free!' " read Debby. She roared in a loud voice as she read, because the words were big and black on the page.

"We could get a piano for Althy maybe," Bonnie brightened up. "Althy wants a piano. Does it say how to get it, Debby?"

Debby studied the advertisement.

"It's just what I was afraid of," she complained after a moment. "It's just a trick. First you have to count the dots. Then it says, 'Counts must be accompanied by subscription to magazine. Fifty cents pays for one year and one count. One dollar pays for two years and three counts. You get fifty dollars extra if you have three counts. It will pay you to have three.' "

"Better look for something else," advised Bonnie. "Here's something."

4

Debby followed Bonnie's finger that pointed to the word "free" underneath the picture of a horse.

"Oh!" she sighed. "That's Dan Patch. 'Free picture of Dan Patch, the world's most famous racing horse!'" she read. "'It shows Dan flying through the air with every foot off the ground. Picture, in six brilliant colors, absolutely free with every order of stock food.'"

"Hmm-m-m!" said Bonnie.

She began looking again.

"What's this?" she asked, pointing to another free offer.

"'Free post cards with your name written on each one in gold,'" read Debby.

"Oh, I'd love my name in gold on a post card!" sighed Bonnie, "I'd just love it! Wouldn't you, Debby?"

"Your name on a post card won't make you rich," Debby told her. "Not even if it's written in gold." And Debby measured the length of her clover chain around her neck.

In a few moments Bonnie sat upright. Her voice tingled with excitement.

"Listen to this, Debby!" she said. " 'Earn one d-o-l-l-a-r, dollar.' "

Quickly Debby laid aside the chain again and read the advertisement. " 'Earn one dollar. Sell twenty of our beautiful colored pictures at ten cents each. Every home wants one. You collect two dollars. Send us one. You keep one.' "

"You don't have to subscribe to anything?" asked Bonnie.

"It doesn't say so."

"Nor buy anything?"

"No."

"Let's see it."

Bonnie read the advertisement, pointing out each word with her finger.

"And look here, Debby!" she cried as her eyes wandered farther down the page. " 'Sell s-e-n-s-a-t-i-o-n-a-l—' "

" 'Sensational,' " Debby said, taking the magazine and reading. " 'Sell sensational new bluing! Try it yourself. Sell it to your friends. We send you twenty packages. Sell them at ten cents each. Collect two dollars. Send us one. You keep one.' "

"You don't have to subscribe to anything?" asked Bonnie.

"It doesn't say so."

"Nor buy anything?"

"No."

"What's 'sensational,' Debby?"

"I think that means whiter than snow," said Debby. "The bluing makes your clothes whiter than snow."

"How do you get the bluing?" asked Bonnie. "And the pictures?"

"You have to fill out the coupons with our names and address, and send for them," Debby told her. "Let's sell them together, Bonnie, shall we? I'll go to the house and fill out the coupons right now if you'll carry in my share of the stove wood. Then we can go across the river to Mr. Flinchum's store and mail the letters."

"People who don't want pictures will be sure to want bluing, won't they?" said Bonnie, her wide eyes sparkling as she got up from the grass and started toward the wood lot.

"And people who don't want bluing will likely want a picture," said Debby. "Just think, Bonnie! We'll earn two dollars. A dollar for the pictures and a dollar for the bluing. One dollar for you, and one for me."

"A whole dollar!" sighed Bonnie. "What will we do with so much money, Debby?"

"Why, when we have that much money, we'll be rich, of course," said Debby.

When Debby had filled out the coupons and ad-dressed the envelopes, and Bonnie had carried in the stovewood, Mother said they might ride the little mare, Mag, across the river to the post office, which was in one corner of Mr. Flinchum's store. Mother gave Debby four pennies from her egg money with which to buy stamps for the envelopes.

Debby put the bridle on Mag and led her to the front gate. Bonnie held the bridle while Debby climbed to the top of the fence, mounted the mare,

and took the reins in her hands. Then Debby held Mag still while Bonnie climbed to the top of the fence and mounted behind her. In one hand Bonnie held the envelopes, while with the other she hugged Debby's waist to keep from falling off.

Down the dusty road sauntered Mag. Debby slapped her with the reins. She clucked to her, and kicked her in the ribs with her bare heels to make her gallop. But Mag only paced a few steps and slowed down to a walk.

"When we earn our money, we'd better pay Mother four pennies of it for stamps," said Bonnie.

"Or we could set the supper table every day," said Bonnie.

"We already set the supper table every day," said Debby.

"We could set every day without being told," said Bonnie. "Mother would think that was special."

"We'll set it the minute we get home," said Debby. And she clucked to Mag and kicked her in the ribs again to make her gallop. But Mag only paced a few steps and slowed down to a walk. Finally, she

splashed across the river and up to the porch of Mr. Flinchum's store, where Debby and Bonnie slid off her back. Debby tied the reins to Mr. Flinchum's hitching post.

"Well, well!" said Mr. Flinchum when he saw Debby and Bonnie. "What can I sell you today?"

"We don't want to buy anything," Debby told him.

"We've come to mail some letters," said Bonnie.

"We're sending for something," said Debby.

"We're going to get rich," said Bonnie.

"Well! Well!" said Mr. Flinchum again, and this time he was really surprised.

The next day Bonnie and Debby climbed on Mag and rode across the river to the post office to see if the pictures and the bluing had come.

"You're in too big a hurry to get rich," teased Mr. Flinchum. "Pictures and bluing are slow travelers. They won't come for several days. For a week. Maybe two weeks."

Debby and Bonnie decided they would wait a week before riding back again. But the next afternoon Bonnie thought they ought to ride Mag over and see if Mr. Flinchum hadn't been mistaken.

Every day for ten days they rode over to the post office. And for ten days there was no sign of a package.

"Nothing but a snail could travel so slowly as pictures and bluing," Bonnie said to Debby on the eleventh day, as they went riding once more to the post office.

They found Mr. Flinchum weighing sugar for a customer in the back of the store.

"Just walk around and look in the box, girls," he called to them.

Around the counter they went to the little cage where Mr. Flinchum kept the mail. There lay a long, round package. Beside it lay a short, square one.

"Oh, Debby!" said Bonnie. "They've come!"

She snatched up the packages.

"Better be sure they're for us," Debby told her.

Debby looked at the label on the long, round package. "Miss Bonnie Fairchild," it said. She looked at the label on the short, square package. "Miss Deborah Fairchild," it said.

"That's us," said Bonnie.

Without another word, Bonnie tucked the long, round package under her arm and held the short, square one in her hand. Then she and Debby climbed on Mag.

"Hold tight, Bonnie! We're going fast!" said Debby.

She kicked Mag in the ribs and clucked to her, and away they went. She didn't need to kick and cluck, however. Mag always went like the wind when she was headed home.

They couldn't take the time to turn Mag into the pasture. They hitched her at the front gate while

14

they ran for the scissors to open the packages.

"I'll open the pictures," said Bonnie. She began to tear the wrappings from the long, round package. Debby began opening the short, square package.

"Oh!" sighed Bonnie. "Do look, Debby. Look at this!" She held up a picture of three horses, a white one, a sorrel one, and a black one, their heads together, looking over a fence.

"That's a million times prettier than Dan Patch!" said Debby.

"Even with all four feet off the ground," agreed Bonnie.

"And look!" said Debby, picking up the next picture in the roll. "Just look at this, Bonnie."

Hanging to nails in a wall were two braces of wild ducks, heads down, their webbed feet tied together, their beautiful feathers shimmering green and purple, red and gray, and as soft as a puff of wind.

"Oh," said Bonnie, "why did they shoot them? I'd rather have them alive."

"Somebody who likes to hunt ducks will buy this one," suggested Debby.

"And look at this one!" cried Bonnie, holding up the next picture, a bowl of fruit. "Every home will surely want one of these, all right. I'd like one, I know. But I like the horses best."

Hurriedly they glanced through the rest of the pictures, but found them all like the first three—horses, ducks, and fruit.

"Let's see the bluing," said Bonnie.

Debby opened the box, and turned it upside down. Out fell twenty small envelopes. Bonnie lifted the flap of one package. Inside were twenty little sheets of dark blue paper.

"Humph!" said Bonnie. "Bluing comes in a box. You have to sprinkle it out. I don't believe this is bluing."

"This is different," Debby told her. "Have you forgotten it's sensational?" She began reading the directions on the envelope. "It says here just to put one of these sheets in the rinsing water," she said, "and the bluing comes right off. Then you have

exactly enough. No guessing. Not too much. Not too little. Too much streaks the clothes with blue. Too little leaves them yellow. This is just right."

After supper Mother and Father, Althy, Chris and Emmy gathered around to see the pictures and the bluing.

Chris thought the picture of the ducks the most beautiful picture he had ever seen. He'd give a hundred dollars for that one, he said, if he had it. But he didn't have even a dime.

Althy liked the bowl of fruit. It was just the picture to put on a dining-room wall, she said. If only she could spare ten cents she'd buy it.

Emmy liked the horses. But she couldn't buy it because she hadn't sold her chickens. In fact, her chickens hadn't even hatched.

Father said their home needed a new picture, and he would buy one. He asked Mother to choose one.

Mother chose the picture of the horses. Right away Father tacked it over the mantel.

Mother said she was almost out of bluing, and she would buy a package of the bluing papers. She said,

too, that the little peddlers selling pictures and bluing up and down the river needed a purse to put their money in. Father found an old leather purse in his dresser drawer. Mother tied a long stout string to the metal fasteners so that Debby might carry it across her shoulder.

Father took two dimes from his pocket and put them into the purse. Debby clicked the metal fasteners shut.

Carefully Bonnie rolled up the rest of the pictures and carried them upstairs. She carried the old purse slung from her shoulder.

Upstairs they took their best calico dresses, clean and stiffly starched, from the clothes rack and hung them beside the bed in which they slept together. They looked in the drawer and found hair ribbons to match their dresses. Then they went to bed.

When they were almost but not quite asleep, Bonnie whispered to Debby, "How rich did you say we would be, Debby, when we sell all the pictures? And all the bluing?" she asked.

"We'll have one dollar from the pictures," said

Debby. "And another dollar from the bluing. That makes two dollars. One for you and one for me."

"Umm-m-m!" sighed Bonnie sleepily. "We'll be richer than almost anybody in the world, won't we, Debby?"

2. Little Orphan
Dirtyknees

E arly the next morning, when Bonnie and Debby had dried the breakfast dishes, fed the chickens, turned the cow into the pasture, and swept the kitchen floor for Mother, they started down the road. Bonnie carried the roll of pictures. Debby carried the box of bluing. Across her shoulder was slung the old leather purse with two dimes in it.

The day was warm, and the dust in the wheel ruts of the road was as soft as feathers under their bare feet.

A mocking bird sang to them from a dead limb in the top of a sycamore tree, but they had no time to listen to mocking birds. They were hurrying away to get rich.

A gray squirrel tried to start a game of whoopy-hide with them, because it was a fine morning to play whoopy-hide. He peeped at them from one side of a chestnut tree and flicked his tail, then dashed around the tree, peeped at them from the other side, and flicked his tail. But they had no time for gray squirrels.

A little striped chipmunk, on his way across the road, stopped at sight of them, sat upright in the wheel rut, and wondered where they were going in such a hurry.

A yellow butterfly bobbed down the road ahead of them.

"Why don't you try to catch me?" he seemed to be saying.

But Bonnie and Debby had no time for chipmunks or butterflies. They were hurrying away to get rich.

At the crossroads they took the left fork of the road through the woods until they came to the Sawyers' house. They hurried through the gate and across the yard where bees were buzzing in and out among Mrs. Sawyer's old-fashioned yellow roses. Shep, the Sawyers' dog, was lying on the back porch. He stood up and wagged his tail at them. Bonnie scratched his head as they went into the kitchen.

Mrs. Sawyer looked up from the new green beans she was stringing.

"Why, good morning, Bonnie and Debby," she said. "Aren't you out pretty early in the morning?"

"We're selling things," Debby told her.

"Pictures," said Bonnie.

"And bluing," said Debby.

"Now, just imagine two little peddlers like you selling things up and down the river!" laughed Mrs. Sawyer. "What kind of pictures are they? And what sort of bluing?"

"Every home wants one of the pictures," explained Bonnie, as she began unrolling them.

"The bluing is sensational," said Debby. "It makes your clothes whiter than snow."

The Sawyer boys and girls heard voices in the kitchen and came hurrying to see who was there. Mr. Sawyer stopped in the kitchen to get a drink of water before going to the cornfield to plow.

Carefully Bonnie and Debby held up the pictures for the Sawyers to see. The Sawyers said "Oh-h-h!"

25

when they saw the three horses looking over the fence. They said "Ah-h-h-h!" when they saw the ducks hanging on the wall. And when Bonnie held up the picture of the bowl of fruit, Mrs. Sawyer said, "That's the one I must have. Have you a dime in your pocket, John, that you can give Bonnie?"

John was Mr. Sawyer. He took a worn old dime from his pocket and handed it to Bonnie. Bonnie dropped the dime into the little black purse, and Debby snapped the fasteners tight.

"This is what the bluing looks like," said Debby, opening the box in her hand and taking a dark blue leaf of paper from one of the envelopes. "It's sensational," she reminded Mrs. Sawyer.

But Mrs. Sawyer had bought a box of bluing at Mr. Flinchum's store only the day before and didn't need more bluing just then.

Debby put the bluing back into the box. Bonnie rolled up the pictures. Debby said she guessed they'd better go.

"What's your hurry?" asked Mr. Sawyer. "Why can't you spend the day?"

"You can at least stay for dinner," said Mrs. Sawyer.

"I found a nest of baby rabbits in the clover field last night, Bonnie," said Jack Sawyer. "Want to see them?"

"I'm making my doll a new dress, Debby," said Janie Sawyer. "You can help me."

But Bonnie and Debby couldn't stay. They said good-by and hurried away down the road.

They walked and they walked. Through the woods and over a high hill the road led them. On the other side of the hill lived Mr. and Mrs. Tribble.

When they reached the Tribbles' house, Bonnie and Debby walked right into the kitchen, but Mrs. Tribble was nowhere around. They looked for her in the front of the house, and in the yard, and in the garden. But they couldn't find her.

"There's Mr. Tribble," said Debby. "See him? There in the stable?"

They stood in the yard a moment watching Mr. Tribble. He was acting strangely. First they saw him kneeling in the dim stable breezeway between the

rows of stalls, bending over something. Then he came outside, shaded his eyes with his hands, and looked toward the house. Then he went back inside the stable, and knelt again.

"We'd better see what's the matter," said Debby.

Carrying the bluing and the pictures, they hurried to the stable. At the stable door they stopped and peeped in. Mr. Tribble had his back to them.

"You poor little lamb!" he was muttering. "You poor little orphan tike of a lamb!"

"What's the matter, Mr. Tribble?" asked Debby.

The sound of her voice startled him. He turned around quickly.

"Oh!" he said. His face was serious. "I thought you might be Amy." Amy was Mrs. Tribble. "Amy went across the mountains to see her sister today, and as soon as she gets out of earshot, my ewe sheep has this little tike of a baby here and then dies and leaves him an orphan."

"Ah-h!" sighed Bonnie. She dropped to her knees beside Mr. Tribble and laid her hand gently on the little newborn lamb that lay on a bed of clean hay.

29

"Poor little tike!" soothed Debby. "Poor little orphan tike!" She knelt beside Bonnie and stroked the lamb ever so gently. "What are you going to do with him, Mr. Tribble?" she asked.

Mr. Tribble shook a troubled head before he replied. "We'll have to be his mother, I guess," he said. "We three."

"We'd better feed him then, hadn't we, Mr. Tribble?" asked Bonnie.

"That we had," agreed Mr. Tribble. "Debby, you run to the house and lift the lid on that box underneath the kitchen window. You'll find some clean rags in it. Bring a piece of an old sheet quick. And bring the pitcher of molasses and a teaspoon from the kitchen table."

Carefully Debby laid the box of bluing in a safe place in the cow stall.

"You'll find an empty medicine bottle on the kitchen shelf, Debby," said Mr. Tribble. "Bring that too."

Debby ran to the house as fast as she could go.

"You take care of the little orphan, Bonnie, till Debby gets back," said Mr. Tribble. "I'll have to round up some breakfast for him."

Bonnie laid the roll of pictures in the cow stall beside the bluing. Then she sat on the stable floor and gathered the wobbly lamb into her arms.

"You poor little tike! You poor little orphan tike!" she crooned to him, over and over. She patted his creamy white fleece that was still damp. She touched

the tip of his sharp black ears ever so gently with her finger. She held him close to her and felt his little, wet, black nose against her neck.

"Look!" she said, pointing to the black patches on his knees as she laid him back on the hay. "You look as if you got your knees dirty, don't you? You're Little Orphan Dirtyknees. That's what you are."

Debby came running from the house with the old sheet, the bottle, the molasses, and the teaspoon. Mr. Tribble came from the pasture, where he had been milking the cow into the kittens' pan.

"He's got a name, Mr. Tribble," said Bonnie.

"So soon?" said Mr. Tribble. "What is it?"

"Little Orphan Dirtyknees," said Bonnie.

"All right, Dirtyknees," said Mr. Tribble. "Your breakfast is on the way."

He poured milk from the pan into the bottle. He added a few drops of molasses. Then he tore a square from the old sheet, folded it, and tied it over the mouth of the bottle.

"If Dirtyknees doesn't like his breakfast served this way, we'll try feeding him with the teaspoon," he said as he worked.

He shook the bottle hard.

"Here Dirtyknees," he said. "Here's your sugar teat."

"Um-m, Dirtyknees! A sugar teat! That's good!" Bonnie told him.

With his finger Mr. Tribble opened the lamb's mouth and put the sugar teat on his tongue. But the lamb didn't swallow. He only shut his mouth and let the white milk dribble down his little black chin.

"Dirtyknees!" scolded Debby. "That's no way to eat."

"You'll never grow up to make a sheep if you don't swallow, Dirtyknees," warned Bonnie. "You want to be a sheep, don't you?"

Still the milk dribbled down the lamb's chin.

"Let's fool him a little," suggested Mr. Tribble.

With his fingers he lightly and rapidly rubbed the lamb's back and his rump about the roots of his tail.

"That's to make the little tike think his mother is licking him," he explained.

Little Dirtyknees lay quietly tasting the warm milk and feeling the gentle rubbing on his rump. But he did not swallow.

Mr. Tribble shook his head.

"Let me rub him," said Bonnie.

She stroked the lamb's back and his rump with her fingers.

"This way?" she asked Mr. Tribble.

"A little faster," Mr. Tribble said. "Always stroke upward, the way his mother would lick him with her tongue."

Lick, lick, lick, lick, lick, went Bonnie's fingers.

Dirtyknees raised his head. He swallowed.

"See!" cried Bonnie. "See, Mr. Tribble! He's eating now!"

Debby took the bottle of milk from Mr. Tribble and held the sugar teat in Dirtyknees' mouth. Bonnie stroked his fleecy rump. "Eat your breakfast, little Dirtyknees!" she coaxed.

Dirtyknees swallowed again. This time he twitched his tail.

"Well, I'll be switched!" said Mr. Tribble.

When Bonnie tired of stroking, she held the sugar teat in Dirtyknees' mouth while Debby stroked him. Sometimes the lamb swallowed right away. Sometimes he waited a long time before swallowing.

"He's finished an ounce," Mr. Tribble said at last. "That's enough for this time. In a couple of hours he'll want breakfast again."

Dirtyknees stretched. He twitched his little tail. Then he went to sleep.

Mr. Tribble stood watching as Bonnie patted the lamb's head.

"Do you know what I'm thinking?" he asked. "I'm thinking I'll make you girls a present of Little Orphan Dirtyknees."

"Us?" asked Debby. "Really, Mr. Tribble?"

"Well, you see," explained Mr. Tribble, "the corn needs plowing and the hay needs cutting, and I don't

have time to sit and hold a sugar teat in a lamb's mouth. And Amy has so many things to mother already—baby chickens and baby ducks and baby guineas and baby turkeys and baby calves—that I imagine she won't mind not having another baby to look after. So if you want Dirtyknees, you can have him."

"Oh, Mr. Tribble!" sighed Bonnie and Debby. And they both knelt down beside the sleeping lamb and looked lovingly at him.

"Can we take him home now?" asked Debby.

"I think he can stand the trip," said Mr. Tribble. "We'll lay him in Amy's egg basket. Just keep him warm. And feed him every two hours for the next three or four days."

"Then what will we do?" asked Bonnie.

"Why, in a week, you won't know the little tike," said Mr. Tribble. "In about a week get Chris to pen him up in the orchard, and make a little trough for him. Put some corn meal in the trough. Sweeten it with a little molasses. And give him all the warm milk he'll drink. He'll come along all right."

Mr. Tribble brought the big hickory egg basket from the hen house. Debby made a soft bed of hay in it. Bonnie lifted the lamb into the basket.

"I'll carry him," said Debby, picking up the basket and starting toward the road.

"I want to carry him," said Bonnie.

"We can take turns," said Debby. "I'll carry him to the crossroads. You carry him the rest of the way. And thank you, Mr. Tribble," she added, "till you're better paid."

"Thank you, Mr. Tribble, till you're better paid," said Bonnie.

"We'll come over every day or two to let you know

how fast he's growing," said Debby.

"Don't hurry him," advised Mr. Tribble. "Give him time to grow. Feed him well and keep him warm. And let him sleep a lot."

At Mr. Tribble's house Bonnie stopped short.

"The pictures!" she cried. "And the bluing! We forgot them."

"I'll wait while you run for them," said Debby.

"What's that you've got?" asked Mr. Tribble as Bonnie came running from the stable with the roll of pictures and the box of bluing.

"It's pictures and bluing we're selling," Debby explained. "We're going to get rich."

"Every home wants one of the pictures," Bonnie told him.

Dirtyknees stirred and stretched in the hickory egg basket. Bonnie peeped at him. He opened his eyes a slit and looked at her.

"You want to get home in a hurry, don't you, little orphan?" crooned Bonnie. "I don't believe your home needs a picture, Mr. Tribble," she added.

"Well, now, maybe it doesn't, maybe it doesn't," agreed Mr. Tribble. "But it does need some bluing. I heard Amy say just this morning she was almost out."

Quickly Bonnie took a package of bluing from the box and handed it to Mr. Tribble. "It's sensational," she told him.

Mr. Tribble fished in his pocket until he found a shiny new dime and gave it to her. She put it in the old purse with the other three dimes, clamped the fasteners shut and picked up the roll of pictures and the bluing.

"Good-by, Mr. Tribble!" called Debby over her shoulder.

"Good-by, Mr. Tribble!" called Bonnie.

"Good-by! And good luck!" called Mr. Tribble from the porch.

"Remember, Debby," said Bonnie. "At the cross-roads I get to carry Dirtyknees."

3. Old Mrs. Whitaker's Attic

A week went by. Every morning, as soon as Debby and Bonnie had dried the breakfast dishes, fed the chickens, turned the cow into the pasture, swept the kitchen floor, and fed Little Orphan Dirtyknees his breakfast, they started down the river road.

They trudged over hills and into hollows, showing their pictures and their bluing at every house. And every noontime when they came home, they had another dime in the old purse.

On Friday afternoon they started to Old Mrs. Whitaker's house. Chris promised to feed Dirtyknees for them if they weren't home on time.

Old Mr. Whitaker and Old Mrs. Whitaker lived far away around the hills and down the hollows. They were so old that they seldom left home. Debby had seen them twice, but Bonnie had seen them only once.

Bonnie and Debby had never seen Old Mr. Whitaker's house. They had only seen signs of it. One winter morning when they were climbing the mountain on the way to school, they turned and looked far down the river. At the tip end of a long, narrow hollow, they saw a thin column of blue smoke curling up above the bare treetops.

"That's smoke from Old Mrs. Whitaker's fire," Chris told them. "She's getting dinner."

Another morning when Bonnie thought she caught a glimpse of something white fluttering in the wind, Althy told her, "That's Old Mrs. Whitaker's wash on the line. Her sheets are dancing a jig in the wind."

"Maybe Old Mr. Whitaker's playing them a tune on his old fiddle," suggested Emmy. "Maybe the sheets are do-ci-doing to his fiddle music."

It was the middle of the afternoon when Bonnie and Debby reached the Whitakers' house. They were surprised to see that it was such a big house. It had turned the color of silver in the sun and wind and rain. Windows with many panes of glass looked quietly down on them. In the afternoon sun they looked silver, like the house.

The front door was standing open. Bonnie wondered if they shouldn't knock to let Old Mrs. Whitaker know they were there.

"That would seem like we're strangers," Debby whispered to her.

They went around the house and straight to the big kitchen. There in a hickory rocking-chair on one side of the door sat Old Mrs. Whitaker rocking

43

herself and resting. In a little straight chair tilted back against the wall, on the other side of the door, sat Old Mr. Whitaker, smoking his corncob pipe and resting.

"Why, bless my soul! Aren't you the little Fairchild girls?" chirped Old Mrs. Whitaker at the sight of Bonnie and Debby standing in her kitchen doorway. She got up to meet them.

"Why, bless my soul *and* body!" said Old Mr. Whitaker, taking his pipe out of his mouth and squint-

35

44

ing at them over his spectacles. "What are your names?" He got up and hobbled toward them on his cane.

"I'm Debby," said Debby.

"I'm Bonnie," said Bonnie.

"How did you find your way so far from home?" Old Mrs. Whitaker asked. She chirped as gaily as a robin when she talked. She did not wait for Debby and Bonnie to answer her questions.

"Timothy, you hurry and bring some milk from the spring. They must have a cold drink right away," she said. "Put your packages there on the table, girls. Here's a chair for you, Bonnie. Here's one for you, Deborah. This very morning when the rooster crowed in the kitchen door three times, I said to Timothy I said, 'That's a sure sign company's coming, and I'll stir up some ginger cookies right now.' But we never thought we'd be having such fine company as this."

Bonnie and Debby sat in the chairs Old Mrs. Whitaker brought them, and drank the cold sweet milk and ate the good ginger cookies. And all the while Old Mrs. Whitaker and Old Mr. Whitaker

eyed them with their robin-bright eyes and asked them questions, poured more cold milk in their mugs and passed them ginger cookies.

"I like your kitchen," said Debby.

Indeed, it was a kitchen anybody would like. It was big and sunny, and open to the breezes that swept cleanly through it. It was scrubbed and spic and span from top to bottom. In a bird cage near a window a yellow canary sang until it seemed as if he would burst his feathers off. A big gray cat stretched under the table with her two striped kittens crawling over her. On the wall by the door a clock ticked away loudly. Just as Debby was having her fourth cup of milk and Bonnie her sixth ginger cooky, a little door on the clock opened and out popped a little bird.

"Cuckoo! Cuckoo! Cuckoo! Cuckoo!" he sang out.

"What made him do that?" asked Bonnie.

"He's telling you it's four o'clock," explained Old Mr. Whitaker.

"Um-m-m!" sighed Bonnie. "I *do* like your kitchen!"

Old Mrs. Whitaker explained how the cuckoo came out every hour and told them the time of day. Bonnie and Debby told the Whitakers about Dirtyknees.

"And now we must be going as soon as we show

you our pictures and our bluing," said Debby.

She and Bonnie unrolled the pictures while Old Mr. and Mrs. Whitaker came close and squinted at every one of them.

"Every home wants one," said Bonnie.

"Of course! Of course!" agreed Old Mr. Whitaker. "This home hasn't had a new picture in fifty years, has it, Molly? I believe it could use three."

They bought one picture of the horses, another one of the ducks, and another of the bowl of fruit. And they bought, besides, a package of the bluing because Old Mrs. Whitaker said she hadn't been satisfied with the bluing she had been buying lately.

"Why can't you stay to supper?" asked Old Mr. Whitaker when Debby put the four dimes in the purse and rose to go.

"We have to hurry home to feed Dirtyknees," explained Debby.

"We had to feed him every two hours at first," said Bonnie.

"Could your brother feed him for you tomorrow,"

asked Old Mrs. Whitaker, " and you could come back and spend the night with us? It's been a long time since we had two little girls spend the night with us."

"And sleep in your beds?" asked Bonnie.

"We'll ask Mother," said Debby. "I think she'll let us come."

They were so excited that they almost forgot to say good-by to Mr. and Mrs. Whitaker.

The next day was Saturday, and in the middle of the afternoon, Mother, Althy and Emmy stood in the doorway watching as Bonnie and Debby set out

down the road toward the Whitakers' house. Althy had braided their hair neatly, and because this was a special occasion, like Sundays and the Christmas program at the schoolhouse in the woods, she had tied the braids with ribbons. Their faces were scrubbed and shining. They wore their best dresses.

"Good-by!" called Emmy.

"Good-by!" called Althy.

"Good-by, and be good children!" called Mother. "Help Old Mrs. Whitaker with the dishes. And remember your manners."

"Good-by!" called Debby and Bonnie.

Down the road they passed Father and Chris hoeing young corn in the cornfield.

"Good-by!" called Chris. "I'll feed Dirtyknees while you're gone."

"Good-by!" called Father. "Hurry home in the morning."

"Good-by!" called Debby and Bonnie.

They walked and they walked. Over hills and down long dusty hollows they went. When the sun was starting to get low, they came in sight of the old

silvered house where Mr. and Mrs. Whitaker lived. They walked right into the kitchen and found Old Mrs. Whitaker getting supper. Old Mr. Whitaker was in the stable milking.

"I'll set the table for you," said Debby.

"I'll help," said Bonnie.

Mrs. Whitaker showed them where to find the plates, the knives and the forks. It had been a long time, she told them, since she had had two little girls to set the table for her.

"I have some special plates for you," she said. Going to a cupboard, she took two plates from the top shelf. On one was the picture of an old castle standing high on a cliff beside a swiftly flowing river.

"This one is for you, Deborah," she said. She called Debby Deborah. "And this one is for you, Bonnie." She handed Bonnie a plate with a picture of Indians wearing long feathers in their hair.

"Oh!" sighed Bonnie. "I've never eaten my supper off of Indians!"

When the table was set, Bonnie and Debby played with the kittens, looked at their plates, and watched for the cuckoo in the clock.

"He's coming out in a minute now," warned Old Mrs. Whitaker.

Suddenly the little door opened. Out popped the little bird.

"Cuckoo! Cuckoo! Cuckoo! Cuckoo! Cuckoo!" he sang.

"Five o'clock!" sang Debby.

At suppertime Old Mr. Whitaker kept their plates filled with new potatoes and green beans, with hot biscuits and honey, and Old Mrs. Whitaker kept their mugs filled with milk until they could neither eat another bite nor drink another sip.

"Thank you for the supper," said Debby, when they finished. "Thank you for the supper," said Bonnie. "We'll help you wash the dishes."

When the dishes were washed, Old Mrs. Whitaker

said she wanted to show them the house. Up the stairs they climbed. They looked in every room along the hall.

"This was Hatty's room and Jenny's," said Old Mrs. Whitaker at the door of the first room. "Next was Mary's and Cappie's. Next to theirs was John's and Sebastian's. And this was Peter's and Jimmy's," she said at the door of the fourth room.

"Were they your children?" asked Debby.

"Yes, they were my children," smiled Old Mrs. Whitaker. "All eight of them."

"Where are they now?" asked Bonnie.

Old Mrs. Whitaker smoothed a wrinkle out of the bedspread on Peter and Jimmy's bed. "Don't you know how birds fly out of the nest when they're old enough to try their wings?" she asked. "Well, our eight children have all flown out of the nest. They're scattered now. They've built their own nests. But once in a while they come back. I keep their rooms ready for them."

"What does this door lead to?" asked Debby, pointing to a closed door in the hallway.

"To the attic," said Old Mrs. Whitaker.

She opened the door. A hot, musty smell greeted them from the top of a steep, dim stairway.

"You may go up there if you want to," said Old Mrs. Whitaker. "Hatty and Jenny and Mary and Cappie used to play up there. How they loved rainy days! On rainy days they dressed up in the old clothes they found in the attic."

Up the steep stairs went Debby, feeling her way, with Bonnie at her heels. At the head of the stairs the smell was even mustier and hotter than at the bottom.

The attic was a long, low room with a tiny window at each end. Dim sunlight from the setting sun fell across the floor. Silken cobweb cradles swung in the corners among the rafters. Mud daubers had built their clay houses up against the ridgepole and against the rafters. Everywhere were old boxes, and bundles of yellowed papers, and little bunches of letters tied with faded ribbons. A carved wooden chest stood against the wall. In one corner of the attic hung old, old dresses, musty-smelling and wrinkled, with yellowed lace at the throats and velvet ribbons at the elbows. Beside them hung stiff, dusty old uniforms that had been worn by some long-ago soldier. Standing in another corner was a rifle as tall as a man. About the room stern women wearing frilly lace caps on their stiff curls, and with lace at their throats, and sterner men wearing powdered wigs

looked solemnly at them out of heavy gold picture frames.

"Let's go, Debby," whispered Bonnie.

"What do you want to go for?" asked Debby. "Look here!"

She pointed to a little wooden cradle, soft and mellow with age. The rockers were worn with the

prints of many a foot that had rocked it.

"Old Mrs. Whitaker must have rocked her eight babies in this," said Debby.

Bonnie looked closely at the cradle.

"Look, Debby, what I've found!" she cried. She lifted from underneath the patchwork quilt that covered the cradle a battered wooden doll wearing a long

yellowed dress. The dress had once been white, lace-trimmed, and was tucked from top to toe. "Let's take it downstairs and play with it," she suggested.

"Look what we found, Mrs. Whitaker," they said as they went back to the kitchen.

"That's Bridget," said Mrs. Whitaker. "She was my doll. When I was a little girl she went with me everywhere I went. Once, I remember, we got lost."

"Tell us about when you got lost." Bonnie begged.

The sun had set, and it was growing dim in the kitchen. Old Mrs. Whitaker lighted the lamp. One of the kittens curled around Debby's feet as she sat in her chair. The other climbed up into Bonnie's lap, cuddled down beside Bridget, and fell asleep. Outside, in the old oak trees, tree toads made a sore-throated purring sound. Crickets cheeped under the stone steps at the doorway. Across the green grass in the yard, lightning bugs sparkled and danced.

"I must have been four," Old Mrs. Whitaker said.

"Did you live in this house?" asked Debby.

"In this very house. Every afternoon I went with my oldest sister Katy to bring home the cows. One afternoon I was in the orchard playing and didn't hear her call me. When I found she had gone without me, I set out through the woods to catch her. I was sure I knew the way, even though the cows had made many paths among the trees. I took Bridget with me.

"The woods separated the house from the pasture.

59

I hadn't walked far until I came to a fork in the path. I took the fork, and hurried along, expecting to overtake Katy any minute.

"Pretty soon I came to another fork in the path. Then I knew I was on the wrong path. It was getting dark in the woods. I turned back and began to run. I ran and ran, until I came to still another fork— one that I had never seen before. Then I knew I was lost. And all the while the woods had grown darker and darker."

"Why didn't you call Katy?" asked Bonnie. "I go with Althy for the cows, and whenever I'm lost, I always call her."

"I was afraid Indians might hear me," said Old Mrs. Whitaker. "Indians prowled in the woods then, and wolves and bears and panthers."

"Why couldn't you find your way home?" asked Debby.

"By that time it was very dark, and I must have gone around and around in a circle in the woods. I stumbled against the roots of trees. I scratched my legs and tore my clothes on bushes. Bridget tore her clothes, too. See where they're mended? My mother mended them."

"Why didn't your mother and your father come and look for you?" asked Bonnie.

"Oh, my dear, they did. Soon after dark I heard someone calling. I was sure it was my mother calling me, and I started in the direction of her voice. Then I remembered that panthers make a noise like a woman calling someone. I told myself it might not be my mother calling. It might be a panther. And I was so frightened that I began to cry—but softly, mind you! I didn't make a sound. And I hurried through the woods as fast as I could, away from the screaming."

"Was it a panther screaming?" asked Bonnie.

"It was my mother calling me. But I was afraid. And I went farther and farther into the woods, crying and crying, and hugging Bridget hard for fear I might lose her.

"After a while I came to a clearing in the woods. There was no moon, but I still remember how bright the stars were, and how close they were hanging over

61

the clearing. I sat down against a tree and must have fallen asleep. But soon I heard a terrible noise in the woods behind me.

"Thump! Thump! Thump! And after a while, Thump! Thump! Thump! Thump! Between thumps there was a whooshing noise in the woods."

"Was that a panther?" asked Bonnie, gripping the edge of her chair.

"That must have been a bear," said Debby.

Old Mrs. Whitaker shook her gray head and smiled.

"If only I could have known!" she said. "It was a searching party out looking for me. They were

thumping the trees to find the hollow ones, for a wild animal could have carried me into a hollow tree and hidden me there, you know. The whooshing I heard was the noise the men made as they tramped through the woods. They would tramp a distance, stand still and listen, then tramp again.

"I thought it was a pack of wolves tracking me down. I was so scared I don't know how I ever got to my feet. But I managed to somehow, and ran across the little clearing. I remember stubbing my toe hard just as I reached the woods on the other side. But I didn't know anything else until I woke up. It was daylight. I was lying in my mother's big bed, and Mother was bending over me, rubbing my hands and feet, and trying to force hot milk down my throat."

"Just the way we feed Dirtyknees," smiled Bonnie, sitting back in her chair again.

"The house was full of people," said Old Mrs. Whitaker, "tiptoeing in and out, and looking at me, and telling my mother what to do.

"It was a few minutes after I awoke before I could remember what had happened. Then I looked on the pillow beside me. I raised the covers and looked on the pillow beside me. I raised the covers and looked underneath. Then I began to cry. This time I was safe inside the house, and could cry as loud as I wanted to. And how I cried! I almost raised the roof right off the attic! I screamed and screamed, and brought everybody running and bending over me, trying to understand what I was saying."

"You'd lost Bridget," guessed Debby.

"I'd lost Bridget," said Old Mrs. Whitaker. "And the harder I cried, the less I could talk. Finally my mother understood what I was saying. She told my father, and my father told the rest of the men who were standing around the room. Do you know what those men did?"

"What did they do?" asked Bonnie and Debby.

"They organized another search party and found Bridget right in the middle of the clearing where I had dropped her. But her eyes were never the same. See? One of them had been pecked."

Bonnie examined Bridget's eyes. She found small dents in one of them.

"A crow tried to steal her eyes," said Old Mrs. Whitaker.

She got up from her chair. "And now it's time for little girls to be in bed," she said.

"Oh, I'm not sleepy," said Debby.

"I'm not sleepy, either," said Bonnie. "Tell us another story, please, Mrs. Whitaker, about when you were a little girl."

"Some other Saturday night when you come over I'll tell you another story," promised Old Mrs. Whitaker. "Everything in the attic has a story about it."

"The next time you come I'll tell you about my pet sheep, Solomon," said Old Mr. Whitaker.

Bonnie and Debby slept upstairs that night in the big bed where Hatty and Jenny had slept before they grew up and left the nest. Bridget slept on a chair, on a pillow as soft as a feather bed, close beside Bonnie.

65

The next morning Bonnie and Debby hurried downstairs as soon as they heard Old Mrs. Whitaker stirring around in the kitchen. They were careful not to wake Bridget.

"We'll set the table for you, Mrs. Whitaker," said Debby.

"May we eat breakfast from the same plates?" asked Bonnie.

"Oh, my, yes!" said Old Mrs. Whitaker.

66

"You have the prettiest plates in the world," said Bonnie.

"Is there a real castle like this one on my plate?" asked Debby.

"Of course," said Old Mrs. Whitaker. "That's in the old country. My great-grandfather was a wonderful musician. He played the harpsichord in that very castle."

"Are the Indians on my plate the same Indians Mr. Whitaker fought when he wore his uniform?" asked Bonnie.

"An Indian saved Timothy's life one time," said Old Mrs. Whitaker.

"Will Mr. Whitaker tell us that story when we come again?" asked Bonnie.

"I shouldn't be surprised," said Old Mrs. Whitaker. "That one and the story about Solomon too. And he might play the fiddle for you."

When they had eaten breakfast and Bonnie and Debby had dried the dishes for Old Mrs. Whitaker, Debby said they must go home and feed Dirtyknees.

"You must take something with you," said Old Mr. Whitaker.

"Yes, you must," said Old Mrs. Whitaker. She looked about the big kitchen. "How would these do?" she asked. She brought out the old plates, and handed to Debby the plate with the picture of the old castle on it, and to Bonnie the plate with the picture of Indians on it.

"Are these for us, Mrs. Whitaker?" asked Debby.

"To take home with us?" asked Bonnie.

"Of course," said Old Mrs. Whitaker.

"Thank you till you are better paid," said Debby.

"Thank you till you are better paid," said Bonnie. "We'll come back soon."

They said good-by, and Debby and Bonnie started home. Down the road they turned and waved to Old Mr. Whitaker and Old Mrs. Whitaker, who were standing in the kitchen door watching them. They heard the cuckoo clock strike eight.

As soon as they were out of sight of the house they began to walk faster. They were in a hurry to show their plates to Mother and Father, to Althy and Chris and Emmy.

"I think I'll let Chris eat his dinner from my Indian plate," said Bonnie. "He fed Dirtyknees for us."

"And Emmy set the table for us and carried in the stovewood for Mother while we were gone," said Debby. "She can eat dinner from my castle plate."

They climbed a hill and crossed a hollow, Debby in front, carrying her plate with the castle on it, Bonnie following, carrying her Indian plate.

"I wish I could have heard Old Mrs. Whitaker's great-grandfather playing the harpsichord in my castle," said Debby.

"What's a harpsichord, Debby?" asked Bonnie.

"Something like our organ," said Debby.

"I think Althy plays the organ nice," said Bonnie.

"I'll let Althy eat her supper off the castle," said Debby. "She'll like that."

"And Mother and Father can eat their breakfast tomorrow from our plates," said Bonnie. "And after that the plates will be ours for breakfast, dinner, and supper."

"Forever and ever," said Debby. "Till we are as old as Old Mrs. Whitaker.

4. Diddle Diddle Ducklings

L isten to this, Bonnie," said Debby. Bonnie and Debby were in the orchard with Dirtyknees. Chris had built a pen for the lamb in a sunny corner of the orchard. In one corner of the pen Father had stretched a burlap sack across four stakes driven in the ground. Dirtyknees could lie and rest in the shade of the sack when the sun made him too warm.

Chris had made him a trough too. When Debby and Bonnie put Dirtyknees' supper of corn meal in it, he shuffled up on his wobbly legs and sniffled at it. Then he licked it up clean, from one end of the trough to the other. He was learning to drink his milk from a pan too, but he liked best to suck it from a sugar teat.

That day Bonnie was holding the bottle for him. "You little rascal!" she was scolding him. "You ought to learn to drink your milk out of the pan. You'll never grow up till you do. I believe you're going to be spoiled."

"Listen to this, Bonnie," said Debby. She was sitting on the grass reading the advertisements in Mother's new magazine that had come only the day before yesterday. " 'Spend one dollar. Make twelve,' " she read. " 'That's really getting rich!' "

Bonnie jerked the bottle out of Dirtyknees' mouth and hurried to look over Debby's shoulder.

"Baa-aa-aa!" cried Dirtyknees in a high, thin voice.

"I told you you'd have to learn to drink out of a pan," Bonnie scolded him, gently. "We can't stand and feed you all day long, Dirtyknees. We're trying to get rich."

" 'Send one dollar for one dozen Pekin duck eggs,' " read Debby. " 'Guaranteed to hatch. Sell eleven-weeks-old ducklings at one dollar each. Easy money.' We have exactly one dollar, Bonnie, I counted it this morning. We could send for the duck eggs right away, and when we sell the ducks, we'll be richer than Althy or Chris or Emmy."

"How rich will we be?" asked Bonnie.

"Awfully rich," said Debby. "We'll have twelve dollars. You take half and I'll take half."

"How much is half?" asked Bonnie.

"Look," said Debby. She plucked twelve clover heads and laid them in a row. "You take one, then I'll take one," she said.

Bonnie took a clover head, then Debby took a clover head, until all the clover heads were gone.

"Now, how many have you?" asked Debby.

"One. Two. Three. Four. Five. Six," counted Bonnie. "Will I have that much—six dollars, Debby?"

"Of course," said Debby.

"And you'll have six dollars too?"

"Of course. And besides, we'll have another dollar when we finish selling the bluing and the pictures."

Bonnie's eyes were wide. "What will we ever do with so much money, Debby?" she asked.

They picked up the magazine and hurried to the house. Dirtyknees looked after them sadly through the cracks in his pen. "Baa-aa-aa!" he cried softly. Then he shuffled to his trough to see if he could find some more corn meal in it.

Mother told Debby what to say in her letter asking for duck eggs. When Debby had written the letter and had folded a dollar inside it, Mother gave her two cents with which to buy a stamp.

"We'll set the table for you as soon as we get back from Mr. Flinchum's," promised Bonnie.

Debby sealed the envelope.

"Maybe we ought to give Mother and Father some of the money we'll make when we sell the ducks," said Debby. "Twelve ducks will gobble up a lot of food in eleven weeks. And think of the corn meal Dirtyknees eats."

"That sounds fair enough," said Mother.

"How much should we pay you?" asked Debby.

"We'll decide later," said Mother. "Sometimes people like to be paid in kindness. Suppose we wait to see how much you make from your ducks."

"Twelve dollars," Bonnie reminded her. "The magazine said so."

Debby and Bonnie climbed on Mag and rode across the river to Mr. Flinchum's store, where they mailed the letter. They told Mr. Flinchum about the ducks, and the twelve dollars they were going to earn. They waited three days. After that, they rode over to Mr. Flinchum's store every day to see if the eggs had come. Finally, one Wednesday afternoon, they saw Mr. Flinchum waiting for them on the porch of the store. Debby kicked Mag in the ribs to make her go faster. Debby wanted her to gallop. But she only paced.

"They've come!" shouted Mr. Flinchum when Bonnie and Debby came near the store. "I know you're in a hurry, so I brought them out to you to save time."

Debby pulled Mag alongside the porch.

"I'll carry them," said Bonnie.

"You want to be careful now," said Mr. Flinchum, as he put the box of heavy cardboard in her hands. "Eggs'll break, you know."

Debby turned Mag's head toward home. Mag began to trot.

"Debby!" screamed Bonnie, bouncing on Mag's back. "Stop her! I can't hold on! I'll break the eggs!"

"Whoa, Mag!" scolded Debby. "Whoa!" She tightened the reins. But Mag only trotted the faster. Debby bounced and Bonnie bounced. "Oh, Debby! The eggs will all be broken!" wailed Bonnie. "I think I hear them breaking now."

Two of the eggs were broken, they found when they opened the box in the kitchen. But Mother told Bonnie she mustn't feel badly about a thing that couldn't be helped. And she couldn't help it if Mag's legs worked like lightning every time she turned her head toward home.

"Anyway, we'll have ten dollars," said Debby. "That's five for you and five for me."

Mother went with them to the hen house where a hen was setting. She put her hand gently under the hen's wings and lifted her from the nest. The hen pecked at her.

Bonnie and Debby laid the big, white eggs into the nest. Mother put the hen on them. The hen settled herself on the eggs, folded her strong wings

about them, fluffed the feathers of her breast over them, and settled down to hatching the ducklings that were to make Bonnie and Debby rich.

Busy days followed. Every day Bonnie and Debby went up and down the river selling pictures and bluing. Every day, three times a day, they fed Dirtyknees, coaxing him to drink his milk from a pan. Every day they played with him in the orchard. He was growing fast now. He no longer wobbled when he walked. His sturdy legs looked like four posts. He bounced after Debby and Bonnie as they played in the tall orchard grass. Sometimes he lowered his little black face and butted them with his head.

"I know something!" sang Bonnie one day, "I know

something Dirtyknees can do."

"What?" asked Debby.

"He can go to school with us one day, like the lamb Mary had."

"We'd have to ask Miss Cora," said Debby.

"She'll let him come," said Bonnie. "She likes lambs. Some Friday afternoon when we're speaking pieces, you can recite 'Mary Had a Little Lamb,' and I'll be Mary. Dirtyknees can follow me into school. Won't Miss Cora like that?"

"Everybody will like that!" agreed Debby. "But we'll have to teach Dirtyknees some manners."

"He is an awful butter," said Bonnie. "Do you suppose we could teach him not to butt?"

"We could try," said Debby. She looked at Dirtyknees, who was starting in her direction with his head lowered. "But it will probably take all summer," she said, dodging him.

Mother said it would take four weeks for the duck eggs to hatch. Debby counted four weeks on the calendar and made a circle with her pencil around July 15, which was the end of four weeks. Every day

she and Bonnie looked at the calendar. It took so long to get to July 15! Sometimes they went to the hen house to watch the hen, but they didn't touch her because she pecked very hard when she was disturbed. They kept fresh water in a pan near her, and scattered corn beside the pan. Twice when they found her off the nest, they sprinkled the eggs with warm water to help the ducklings hatch.

At last July 15 came. Early in the morning, as soon as Bonnie and Debby had dried the breakfast dishes, fed the chickens and Dirtyknees, turned the cow into the pasture, and swept the kitchen floor, they hurried to the hen house. Mother went with them.

The hen stirred on her nest.

"I believe they're beginning to hatch," said Mother.

She eased her hand gently under the hen. This time the hen didn't peck. She only scolded softly.

"Look!" said Mother.

Bonnie and Debby peeped into the nest. Beneath Mother's hand lay one egg with the shell pipped. Out of it wriggled a yellowish, wet head with a long, flat bill and two tiny eyes set high above.

"Oh-h-h!" whispered Bonnie. "It's alive!"

Mother pulled away her hand gently and let the hen settle again.

"We'll come back later," she said. "We'll have to keep the shells cleaned out of the nest as the ducklings hatch."

"When can we take them off?" asked Debby.

"Not till morning," said Mother. "They must all hatch and have time to dry."

The next morning, before the dishes were washed, the chickens were fed, the cow was turned into the pasture, or the kitchen floor was swept, Debby and Bonnie hurried to the hen house, carrying Mother's egg basket warmly lined with rags.

Dirtyknees baaed at them from the orchard.

"You'll have to wait for your breakfast this morning, Dirtyknees," Bonnie called to him. "You can wait just this once, can't you?"

Inside the hen house the hen sat on her nest. One little yellow head poked out from underneath her right wing. Two heads poked from beneath her left wing. A tiny webbed foot was thrust from underneath her warm breast. She was pushed and shoved gently this way and that by the ten downy bodies in the nest.

Mother lifted the hen off the nest.

"Oh-h-h!" cried Bonnie, "Look!"

Up bobbed ten golden heads. Ten pairs of bright eyes blinked at the light. Ten yellow bills opened.

"Queek! Queek!" said the ducklings through their noses.

Bonnie and Debby lifted them into the basket, one at a time. The ducklings squirmed, and fluttered their

tiny wings. They were warm and soft. They spread their webbed feet and teetered on Debby's fingers.

"Oh, Debby, do be tender with them!" warned Bonnie.

Debby covered the ducklings with rags to keep them warm, and carried them to the lower end of the orchard where Father had made a pen for them. Mother carried the hen.

Inside the pen on a rise of ground was a sycamore tree. Underneath the tree Father had made a house

for the hen and the ducklings. On the floor of it lay a carpet of clean, dry straw. For the length of the pen ran the stream of clear water that skirted the orchard.

Debby and Bonnie lifted the ducklings from the basket and put them into the house. Mother set the hen in the house too. With great fussing and cluck-ing and scratching in the straw, she gathered all ten of her children underneath her wings and snuggled them up to keep them warm. No sooner had she got them settled, however, when from underneath her breast popped a downy head. "Queek!" said the duck-ling.

"Look!" said Bonnie. "As soon as its mother gets it tucked into bed, it says, 'Mother, I want a drink of water.' "

"They'll find their water soon enough," said Mother. "It won't be long before they decide to go for a swim. But you and Debby must come to the house now and get some breakfast for them."

In the kitchen Mother crumbled stale bread into a pan and moistened it with skimmed milk.

"Tomorrow you can add a pinch of sand to their food," she said. "They'll need sand for about a week. Then they'll be old enough to eat all sorts of good things—chopped dandelion greens, and chopped clover, and little bits of lettuce, and oatmeal. Ducklings like charcoal, too, when they're a little older."

"Sand and charcoal!" laughed Bonnie. "How would you like to be a duck, Debby?"

They hurried back to the duck pen with the pan of breakfast and set it near the house. Out of the house came the mother hen, clucking to the ducklings to follow. One by one they scrambled after her, made their way with her to the pan, and dipped their flat, yellow bills into the bread. They thrust up their bills, swallowed, and dipped in for more.

Dirtyknees was baaing from his pen at the top of the orchard. He couldn't understand why Debby and Bonnie didn't come to play with him. They had little time to play with Dirtyknees that day, however. They fed him his breakfast and romped through the grass with him for a minute, and warned him not to butt if he wanted to go to school with them. Then they shut him in his pen again.

"Baa-aa-aa! Baa-aa-aa!" he cried.

Bonnie shook her finger at him. "Dirtyknees, you're just a spoiled baby," she declared. "Don't you know we have other babies to take care of right now? We'll come back later and play with you."

"You be practicing your manners, Dirtyknees, while we're busy," Debby told him.

Bonnie and Debby did not go up and down the river that day selling pictures and bluing. They were too busy.

In the middle of the afternoon, when they were sitting quietly in the duck pen, a yellow head peeped from beneath the hen's wing. A tiny webbed foot was thrust out, followed by a little fluttering wing. All at once the duckling freed himself, stretched his

wings, and started waddling down the slope toward the stream.

Out came another duckling. And another. And another. Finally all ten of them were free. A long, downy, yellow line they made waddling down the slope.

"Debby! Look where they're going!" cried Bonnie.

At the edge of the stream the first duckling lifted his wings, gave himself a little shove, and launched himself like a small boat on the cool, clear water. Out launched another. And another, until ten ducklings went paddling downstream.

Down to the bank of the stream fluttered the mother hen. She clucked and clucked. She ran down

the stream and clucked. She ran up the stream and clucked. She fluttered and fluttered and clucked some more.

"Don't worry," Debby said to her. "Your children will be back."

"Maybe they'll swim away," suggested Bonnie. "Maybe they'll keep on swimming and swimming till they get to the ocean, and never come back."

The mother hen was afraid of that too. She had never before had children who took to water, and she scolded and clucked and fluttered some more.

Bonnie began to call the ducklings. "Di-i-i-i-ddle, diddle, diddle, diddle, diddle, diddle, diddle!" she called. She made a song of the call, her voice at first high, then low as the words came faster.

The duckling at the head of the line made a circle in his course. The others followed. Upstream they paddled, their downy bodies rocking on the ripples.

When they reached the roots of the sycamore tree, they climbed out of the stream, shook the waterdrops from their bodies, and waddled back to their house, the hen scolding them all the while.

"We have to sell them in eleven weeks," Debby reminded Bonnie.

Bonnie did not reply right away. She caught one of the ducklings, smoothed the down on his head, and ran her fingers down his back. She held her hand on the ground and let another put his webbed foot in it. His toes tickled. She let another peck at her finger.

"I don't think I'll sell mine," she said.

"You won't get rich if you don't sell them," Debby reminded her.

"I don't care," said Bonnie.

One afternoon when the ducklings were two weeks

old, Debby and Bonnie set out down the road with their pictures and their bluing. Father and Chris went across the mountain to help Mr. Watterson and Andy get in their hay. Mother went across the river to help Aunt Cassie make jelly. Althy and Emmy went to pick blackberries in the hollow. Nobody was left at home.

In the middle of the afternoon while Debby and Bonnie were at Mr. Tribble's, resting and telling him that Dirtyknees might go to school with them one day in the fall, a cloud came up in the sky. At first it was no bigger than Mr. Tribble's hand. But it began to grow. It grew bigger and it grew darker. It grew angry-looking. It began to flash lightning and to roar thunder. Finally it covered the whole sky, and the earth was dark, and rain began to fall.

Mrs. Tribble lighted the lamp in the kitchen to drive away the darkness.

Bonnie was troubled. So was Debby.

"What will happen to the ducks?" asked Bonnie. "And Dirtyknees?"

"Oh, Dirtyknees will be all right," Mr. Tribble said.

"He's big enough to take care of himself now. And the ducks have their mother with them. She'll tell them what to do."

"They don't mind her very well," Bonnie told him.

"They're pretty headstrong," said Debby.

For an hour the big rain fell out of the dark clouds. The trees drooped their leafy branches with the weight of it. Little rivers ran off the housetop and down the waterspout into Mrs. Tribble's rain barrel. Then, when the rain had drenched the earth, it stopped as suddenly as it had started. The clouds began to scatter. The sun came out, and in the east from one mountaintop to another a double rainbow spanned the sky.

"That means the rain is over," said Debby. "Let's go, Bonnie."

They set off down the road for home as fast as they could go. Mother was there ahead of them. Althy and Emmy were coming from the pasture from the direction of the Huffs' house where they had taken shelter from the storm. Father and Chris came driving home in the wagon.

Down to the orchard ran Debby and Bonnie.

"Baa-aa-aa! Baa-aa-aa-aa!" complained Dirtyknees as they paused a minute to see if he was all right. To be sure, he was about as wet as a lamb can ever be. Debby said she could wring water out of his wool. And he was cross.

"Baa-aa-aa-aa-aa!" he bleated, and butted Bonnie's knees.

"There's nothing wrong with you that can't be made right again," Bonnie scolded him. "You can wait, Dirtyknees, like a good lamb, till we see about the ducks."

Down the orchard hill they ran.

"Di-i-i-i-i-ddle, diddle, diddle, diddle, diddle, diddle, diddle!"

Over and over they called. "Di-i-i-i-i-ddle, diddle, diddle, diddle, diddle, diddle, diddle! Di-i-i-i-i-ddle, diddle, diddle, diddle, diddle, diddle, diddle!"

There was no answer. No yellow downy line came waddling to meet them.

The big wet leaves of the sycamore tree drooped over the ducklings' house. The mother hen was standing near the house, clucking and fussing and walking anxiously about.

Bonnie and Debby climbed into the pen. Under the sycamore tree they stopped. They knew now why the ducks hadn't come when they were called. All ten of them were lying on the wet ground, their bodies limp and chilled, their bright webbed feet limp, their bright eyes half-closed, their soft down matted on their wet bodies in straggling, grayish-yellow wisps.

Bonnie looked at Debby. She began to cry. Debby began to cry too. They cried and they cried. The whole orchard was filled with their crying.

Into her apron Bonnie gathered five of the ducklings. Debby gathered the other five into her apron. Through the wet grass, up the hill, among the apple trees, they made their way to the house. Dirtyknees looked sorrowfully after them as they passed by his pen. "Baa!" he said softly.

Mother met them at the kitchen door. Already she had a fire burning in the stove. A heap of clean rags lay in a chair.

"Wrap them up, children, each one separately," she said. "They'll dry out in no time behind the stove."

Chris and Emmy and Althy came to help them.

Quickly they worked, wrapping each duckling in rags, and laying it carefully behind the warm stove.

Bonnie was still sobbing.

"Will they come back to life, Mother?" she asked.

Mother took one of the ducklings in her hands. Its head dangled from its limp neck.

"I don't know, Bonnie," she said. "But we'll try to bring them back to life. We'll do everything we can."

After supper, until dark, they worked with the ducklings. Mother tried to force them to eat. Debby and Bonnie watched anxiously for any sign of life—any fluttering of wing, any stretching of webbed foot.

At last Mother said it was bedtime. Debby and Bonnie must go to bed, she said. She and Father would work with the ducklings.

Up the stairs went Bonnie and Debby, sobbing.

"Would you like me to come up and tell you a story?" asked Althy.

They thought they would like that. So Althy went up the stairs with them. She sat on the foot of their bed in the dark and told them wonderful stories about the long, long ago until they went to sleep.

Early the next morning they hurried downstairs and into the kitchen.

"We saved one, children," said Mother. "Look behind the stove." There in a box stood one little duckling, as dry as dust, his down fluffy, his eyes bright, eating his stale bread moistened with skimmed milk.

"Where are the others?" Bonnie asked. She knew all along what had happened. But she had made up her mind not to cry any more.

"On the porch, Bonnie," said Mother. "Chris laid the other nine together in a box."

After breakfast Chris helped Debby and Bonnie bury the ducklings in the orchard. They covered the grave with clover blossoms.

5. Hatty One, Hatty Two, Hatty Three

It was very lonely in the duck pen for one small duckling and one mother hen. So Bonnie and Debby moved them to the hen house to live with the chickens.

The duckling liked his new companions. When they sunned themselves in the chicken yard, he sat down and sunned himself. When they climbed on the hen-house roost at night to go to sleep, he squatted in the corner in the clean straw Debby had put there for his bed and shut his eyes. When they wandered about looking for bugs and beetles, he waddled down the orchard hill to the stream and went for a swim. Twice a day when Bonnie came from the stable with a pan full of chicken feed, calling, "Chi-i-i-cky! Chicky! Chicky! Chicky!" the squawking chickens came running and flying toward her and the duckling came waddling behind.

He was growing big and strong now, and the down on his body was losing its golden color.

"We'll have to give him a name," said Debby.

"We could name him 'The Ugly Duckling,' " suggested Bonnie, thinking of the story Emmy had read from her reader at school.

"But he isn't ugly," said Debby.

"We could name him 'The Beautiful Swan,' " suggested Bonnie.

"But he isn't a swan," said Debby.

"We could name him—name him—"

"Why don't we name him Hans?" suggested Debby. "For Hans Andersen, the man who wrote the story about the ugly duckling?"

So they named him Hans, and he was half Debby's, half Bonnie's.

One day they finished selling the pictures and the bluing. Ten dimes were lying in the old purse.

"I'll give you my half of Hans if you'll let me have the ten dimes," said Bonnie to Debby. "Then I'll have a dollar, and you can sell Hans for a dollar. The magazine said so."

"What are you going to do with your dollar?" asked Debby.

"That's a secret," said Bonnie.

"You won't be rich if you spend it," Debby warned her.

"I know," said Bonnie. "But there's something I want more than a dollar. Will you let me have it if I give you my half of Hans?"

Hans waddled by just then on his way to swim.

"I think I'll go and watch him," said Debby. "I like to watch him dive. All right, Bonnie," she added. "I'll keep Hans and you can have the dollar. But I don't believe I'll sell Hans."

Bonnie hurried to the house and found the new mail order catalog that had come the day before yesterday. She turned to a page of hats for girls. In the top corner was pictured the most beautiful hat for girls that Bonnie had ever seen. Its narrow brim was turned up all around. Around the crown was a ribbon with a bow on one side. Above the bow was curled a soft feather. The hat was blue and the feather was red, said the catalog. And the price was one dollar.

Mother helped Bonnie fill out the order blank for the hat. Bonnie sat at the table in Father's chair, with her feet curled around the chair rungs. Whiskers and Jemima, the cats, came and rubbed against her ankles as she wrote.

Bonnie stopped writing and looked down at them. "When are you two going to have some kittens?" she asked them. "I want some baby kittens to play with."

When the order was finished and the dollar sealed inside the envelope, Mother gave Bonnie two pennies with which to buy a stamp. Then Bonnie climbed on Mag and rode over to Mr. Flinchum's store alone to mail her letter. She was in a great hurry. She clucked to Mag, and slapped her with the reins and kicked her in the ribs with her bare heels. She wanted Mag to gallop, but Mag only paced.

It was only after Bonnie mailed her letter and turned Mag toward home that the mare was in a hurry. Then she galloped down the road so fast that Bonnie reached home almost before Mother missed her.

"Now I'll have to begin waiting again," said Bonnie. "The days wouldn't seem so long if we had more pictures and bluing to sell."

"While you're waiting, you can get ready for school," said Mother. "It starts next week, you know."

Mother was very busy making new dresses for Althy, Emmy, Debby, and Bonnie, and new shirts for Chris to wear to school.

"I've already tried on my dresses," said Bonnie, "And I've hunted up my schoolbooks. There's nothing more to do."

"Maybe Dirtyknees would like to play with you awhile," suggested Mother. "He'll get lonesome when you are at school."

So Bonnie went to the orchard to play with Dirtyknees. She raced through the tall orchard grass, and Dirtyknees bounced after her. When he was about to catch her, she climbed an apple tree.

Then he stood underneath the tree and begged her to come down.

"Baa-aa-aa! Baa-aa-aa!" he begged in an almost grown-up voice.

Bonnie slipped down the tree on the other side. Away through the tall grass she ran. Through the tall grass bounced Dirtyknees at her heels.

"You're doing better, Dirtyknees," she told him when finally she stopped to pat him. "You don't butt

quite so hard as you did. I'll ask Miss Cora the very first day if you can come to school. If you're a very good lamb, I'll hunt a ribbon to tie in your wool. How would you like that, Dirtyknees? A red ribbon in your wool?"

"Baa!" said Dirtyknees softly, looking pleased.

When Dirtyknees went back to nibbling grass, Bonnie walked down beside Debby and watched Hans. Hans was paddling downstream. He looked like a big yellow dandelion in the water. When he saw something good to eat in the water, down went his head, and up tipped his tail. Debby thought she'd much rather have him than the swan in the ugly duckling story.

When Bonnie tired of watching Hans, she went to the house and played with the cats.

"When will Jemima have some kittens?" she asked Mother.

Mother was stitching a hem in Emmy's dress. "I shouldn't be surprised if she has some kittens any day now," said Mother.

"Where will she have them?" asked Bonnie.

"You'd better fix a bed for her," said Mother. "Find a box and put some clean rags in it. Put it under the stairs. Jemima will like a warm soft bed to lay her kittens on when they are born."

Bonnie made the bed ready for Jemima's kittens as Mother told her. Then she began to wait for the kittens. She did nothing but wait, she complained. She waited for her new hat. She waited for kittens. She waited for school to begin.

On Friday afternoon before school started, Bonnie and Father rode Mag across the river to Mr. Flinch-um's store. There they found a big box waiting.

"Miss Bonnie Fairchild," Father read the label on the box.

"Oh, Father! Let's hurry home with it. Let's go home faster than we've ever gone before," said Bonnie.

They climbed on Mag again and started home. Father held the box. Bonnie put both arms around Father's waist and held on tight. Away down the road Mag galloped, faster than she had ever galloped before.

Mother, Althy and Chris, Emmy and Debby crowded around to see the new hat as Father cut the string with which the box was tied. Bonnie jerked off the lid. She turned back the tissue paper.

"Ah!" she sighed at sight of the hat. "It's just what I wanted!"

She put it on her head and ran to stand in front of the mirror. The blue brim rolled softly from her light gold hair. The little red feather curled over the crown. It was the most beautiful hat in the world, thought Bonnie.

"May I wear it sometime, Bonnie?" begged Debby. "I'll take good care of it."

It was so beautiful a hat that Bonnie didn't want to give it up.

"You could sell Hans for a dollar, Debby, and buy one for yourself just like it," she said.

Debby shook her head. She couldn't part with Hans, she said. And have him roasted and eaten? She'd rather go bareheaded all her life, she said.

"Sometimes I'll let you wear it," Bonnie promised. But she kept it on her head.

She wore it to the orchard to show to Dirtyknees.

"I can't play with you today, Dirtyknees," she warned him from the gate. "I only want to show you my new hat."

Dirtyknees looked solemnly at the hat. "Baa!" he said.

In the chicken yard Bonnie met Hans.

"Look at my new hat, Hans!" she said.

"Queek!" said Hans through his nose.

In the kitchen Bonnie found Jemima curled in front of the stove.

"See my new hat, Jemima?" she asked.

She didn't wait for Jemima to answer. She hurried to look inside the box under the stairs to see if any kittens had come. But the box was empty, just as she had left it.

110

"When are you going to have those kittens, Jemima?" she scolded, pointing a finger at the cat.

"Meow!" said Jemima.

"You'd better put your hat away and save it for Sunday," said Mother.

Upstairs went Bonnie, wearing the hat and carrying the box in which it came. Debby followed her.

Bonnie set the box on the floor close beside the bed in which she and Debby slept. She took off the hat and laid it carefully in the box. She turned back the tissue paper and stood looking inside. The hat was as dark and as soft as the dark blue sky when the stars are coming out. The feather was redder than the reddest autumn leaf. Bonnie touched the feather with her fingers. She smoothed the soft felt crown with the palm of her hand.

"Aren't you going to cover it up?" asked Debby. "It will get dusty unless you cover it."

"If I cover it, I can't see it," said Bonnie. And she sat on the bed and looked at the hat until Mother called her to set the table for supper.

At bedtime, Bonnie pulled the box close to the

bed on the side where she lay, and looked down at the hat.

"You'd better put the lid on," Debby warned her.

"But I can't see the hat with the lid on," said Bonnie.

"You can't see it anyway when the light is out," said Debby. "And when you are asleep."

"But I want to see it the first thing in the morning," said Bonnie. "The minute I wake up."

The next morning when the sun was just beginning to rise over the mountains, Bonnie awoke. She felt as happy as a lark singing in a meadow. Quickly she turned and looked into the box.

She blinked her eyes. She bent closer and looked. She blinked her eyes again. She tried to swallow, but she couldn't.

She reached her hand cautiously into the box.

Then she burst out crying.

"Debby! Debby! Wake up!" she sobbed, shaking Debby by the shoulder to wake her.

Debby sat up and rubbed her eyes. "What's the matter?" she asked.

"Look what's happened to my hat!" sobbed Bonnie.

Debby leaned across her and looked into the box.

"I can't see," she said, rubbing her eyes again. "What's happened?"

"Jemima's had her kittens right in the middle of my new hat," sobbed Bonnie.

Debby jumped out of bed and stood over the box, looking.

There, in the crown of the new hat, lay Jemima. Beside her in a heap lay three scrawny, squirming kittens, their eyes shut tight, their heads weaving about on their wobbly necks. The soft blue crown of the hat was crumpled flat beneath their bodies. The beautiful feather that was redder than the reddest autumn leaf made a soft pillow for the kittens to lie on.

113

"Why didn't Jemima have her kittens under the stairs?" sobbed Bonnie. "I had her bed all ready for her."

"I guess she liked your hat better," said Debby. Debby felt very sad too. "It was such a pretty hat," she said.

Bonnie wiped her eyes on the sheet, and looked again into the box at the kittens. With her finger she rubbed one of them on the head.

"Their eyes are shut," she said between sobs.

"They'll open them in about a week," Debby told her. "I wouldn't feel too badly about the hat, Bonnie," she added. "It won't be long till winter. And in winter you have to have a warm toboggan cap, or your ears will freeze. You can't wear a hat to school. And you can't wear a hat skating on the river."

"I know," said Bonnie. She wiped her eyes again. "But we haven't any more money," she reminded Debby.

"What does that matter?" asked Debby. "You had one dollar. Now you have three kittens. Three are lots more than one. And besides, Mother will knit you a new toboggan cap this winter. Maybe she'll knit you a blue one with a red tassel on the end of it. And next spring, we can make more money and buy ourselves new hats."

"We can't sell any more pictures," said Bonnie. "Every home already has one. And the bluing lasts a long time."

"There will be other things to sell," said Debby.

Bonnie stopped crying. The hat didn't seem to matter so much any more. She put her finger in the box and rubbed each of the kittens on the head.

"I wish they'd open their eyes," she said. "What shall we name them, Debby?"

Debby thought a moment. "Since they were born in your hat, we might name them Hatty," she said.

"But we can't name them all Hatty," said Bonnie. "There are three of them."

"Hatty One, Hatty Two, Hatty Three," said Debby.

"Since they were born in my hat, that makes them mine, I guess," said Bonnie.

"If I give you half of Hans, will you give me half of the kittens?" said Debby.

"We can have everything together," said Bonnie. "Dirtyknees, and Hans, and Hatty One, Hatty Two, and Hatty Three. Oh, look, Debby!" she cried suddenly. "Look what Jemima's doing!"

Jemima was picking up Hatty One by the scruff of the neck. Hatty One, Debby and Bonnie could see, was going to be a bluish-gray kitten.

With the kitten dangling from her mouth, Jemima sprang out of the hatbox and started downstairs.

"She must have thought we were going to hurt her babies," Debby explained to Bonnie. "Cats always

117

hide their kittens when they think somebody's hurting them."

Debby and Bonnie tiptoed after her. Straight to the box that Bonnie had gotten ready for her under the stairs went Jemima. She laid Hatty One gently on the clean rags.

Up the stairs she raced again. Down she came the second time, carrying Hatty Two, a tiger-striped kitten, with a black band around each eye, like spectacles.

On the third trip Jemima brought Hatty Three, yellowish and mottled like a tortoise shell.

When Jemima had Hatty One, Hatty Two, and Hatty Three safely in bed in the box under the stairs, she lay down beside them and gave them their breakfast. Debby and Bonnie stood watching.

"When *will* they open their eyes?" asked Bonnie.

6. King Strut and Queen Mince

When Mother came to the kitchen to get breakfast she found Bonnie and Debby sitting on the floor beside Jemima's box, looking at the kittens. They told Mother about the hat.

"It's all ruined," Bonnie told her. "The crown is crumpled and the feather is broken and—"

"For shame, Jemima!" scolded Mother. "To ruin a little girl's pretty new hat!"

Mother saw tears gathering in Bonnie's eyes. With her apron she wiped them away.

"I'll tell you what I can do," said Mother. "I have finished making all the new dresses for school. I might as well begin today knitting you a new toboggan cap for winter. How would you like a red and blue one?"

"A blue cap with a red tassel," said Bonnie.

"I think that will look just as pretty on you as the

new hat," said Mother. "I'm going to knit a new cap for you too, Debby. What color would you like? Blue and red like Bonnie's?"

Debby thought this over for a minute. "I'd like green and white, Mother," she said. "A long white cap, as white as snow, and a long green tassel, as green as a pine tree."

"I think I'd like a cap like Debby's instead of red and blue," said Bonnie. "White as snow and green as a pine tree."

"I'll begin knitting them this very day," promised Mother.

Early in the morning Andy Watterson came over to go fishing with Chris. And early in the morning Father saddled Mag and rode away. He was going to the town across the mountains to buy new schoolbooks, new tablets and lead pencils, new slates and slate pencils for Althy and Chris, Emmy and Debby and Bonnie. School was starting on Monday.

Late in the afternoon he came riding home again. Across Mag's back lay a bag filled with the things Father had bought. And in his hand Father carried a big box, tied with a stout string and punched with many holes on each side.

The Fairchilds and Andy hurried to meet him. They crowded around him on the front porch as he opened the bag of books. They took the books, the slates and pencils and tablets he handed them. He brought Andy a new tablet and pencil too. But what everyone most wanted to see was what was inside the big box punched full of holes. There the box sat on the doorstep, looking most mysterious.

Andy put his ear to a hole and listened.

"It's something alive," he said. "I heard it move."

Bonnie put her ear to a hole and listened.

"I heard something step on one foot, then on another," she said.

At last, when there was nothing more in the bag, Father picked up the box.

"Here, Bonnie," he said, "is something for you and Debby. Maybe they will take the place of the ducks that drowned and the hat that Jemima had her babies in."

Bonnie took the box. Debby ran for the scissors with which to cut the stout string.

121

Cautiously Bonnie lifted the lid. They both peeped in.

In one corner of the box, sitting close together, were a bantam rooster and a bantam hen. They were so little that Bonnie could not at first believe they were real. They looked like toys.

She reached her hand inside the box to pet them, and the rooster stood up. He was no match for one of Mother's roosters in size, but he was handsomer than any rooster in the chicken yard. No strutting peacock ever spread finer feathers than the red and bronze feathers, the green and shimmering gold, the rooster wore on his neck, his wings, and his back. His comb was brilliant red, his shimmering green tail was long and arched.

"Oh, Father! Isn't he pretty!" sighed Bonnie. "How could you think of a thing so pretty?"

She lifted the rooster from the box and set him on the floor.

"He's light as a feather!" she said. He wasn't really as light as a feather, but he weighed only a little more than a pound.

Debby lifted the hen from the box and placed her beside the rooster.

123

"She's lighter than a feather!" said Debby. The hen wasn't really lighter than a feather. She weighed a pound exactly. Her comb wasn't so big, but it was just as red as the rooster's. Her feathers weren't so bright as his, but they shimmered in the sunlight.

The rooster clucked softly to the hen. He took a few steps across the porch. The long, arched, green feathers in his tail swept the floor.

Bonnie laughed softly. She didn't want to frighten the rooster.

"Watch him strut!" she whispered. "He's so little. And so proud!"

"He struts like a king," said Andy.

"You can call him King Strut, Bonnie," suggested Chris.

The rooster clucked again, and the hen followed him across the porch. She walked with a haughty air, and with mincing, toy steps.

"And Queen Mince," laughed Debby.

"They can eat with the other chickens," said Father. "But I think we'd better build them a house for themselves."

"About as big as a dollhouse?" asked Bonnie.

"Not much bigger," said Father.

"I'll help," said Bonnie.

"I'll help too," said Debby.

"Andy and I can build it, Father," said Chris.

Debby caught King Strut and Bonnie caught Queen Mince. They put them back in the box and put the lid on it. They didn't want the king and queen to go flying back across the mountains where they came from.

In a corner of the chicken yard Chris and Andy, Debby and Bonnie set to work building a house for King Strut and Queen Mince.

"Since they're a king and queen, we'll have to build them a castle," suggested Andy.

125

Andy and Chris brought planks that were stacked behind the stable. Debby ran for the saw. Bonnie brought the hammer and the nails.

Dirtyknees looked through the cracks of the orchard fence at them. He wondered what they were doing. "Baa-aa-aa! Baa-aa!" he called them softly.

"Be practicing your manners, Dirtyknees," Bonnie called to them. "We'll play with you in a little while."

Hans came waddling up the hill from the stream where he had had an afternoon swim. "Queek!" he said.

"Run along, Hans, and sun yourself," Debby told him. "We'll play with you in a little while."

"We'll play with you tomorrow," Bonnie promised him.

Bonnie stood beside Chris and handed him the nails.

Knock, knock, knock, went the hammer.

Debby held the plank that Andy was sawing. *Whang, whang, whang* went the saw.

Up went the frame of the castle. Up went the walls of the castle. On went the door of the castle. Chris made a special kind of castle door that slid back and forth so that King Strut and Queen Mince might be fastened inside when the weather was bad.

"And when enemies like foxes and weasels are invading their country," said Andy.

The door was almost as tall as the castle, so that King Strut could get his tail inside without bending his feathers.

"It must be a lot of bother to wear a fancy uniform like that all the time," said Chris.

127

On an inside wall of the castle Andy nailed a little box.

What's that for?" asked Bonnie.

"Even kings and queens have to work," said Andy. "You run to the stable loft and bring an armful of clean hay. Then I'll show you."

"I know! I know!" shouted Bonnie. "It's a nest for the queen!"

Chris sawed off the stick of an old broom that he found under the sycamore tree.

"What's that for?" asked Debby.

Even kings and queens have to sleep," said Chris. "Don't you think this looks like a bed?"

"You mean it's a roost," said Debby.

Chris fastened the broomstick in place inside the castle for the king and queen to perch on.

Finally, on went the roof. And there was the castle. But it looked like a playhouse.

"Shouldn't we put a fence around it?" asked Bonnie. "So the King and Queen won't fly away."

"They won't fly away," said Father, who came by just then to see the castle. "They're very tame."

Bonnie put the clean hay in Queen Mince's box. The nest she made was the size of a saucer. She and Debby scattered corn over the ground for the bantams to eat. They filled one small pan with water and another with curds which Mother gave them. Then they brought the bantams from the porch and set them down in front of their castle.

The king strutted about the castle grounds, followed by the mincing queen. They ate a few grains of the corn lying on the ground, drank from the pan

of water, and tasted the curds.

"Is that all they're going to eat?" asked Bonnie. "They eat like toys."

"That's all," said Father. "They have toy appetites. Let's leave them alone now, and let them get used to their new home."

From the back doorstep Bonnie and Debby watched the king and queen. The king never stopped strutting, and the queen never stopped mincing. They strutted and minced when they ran after a beetle that stayed longer than was good for him on a blade of

grass. They strutted and minced when they took a late afternoon walk around their castle. And how they strutted, and how they minced, when Hans waddled past the castle and stopped to see who was living there!

"Poor Hans!" said Bonnie. "He's only trying to be friendly."

"Maybe they're being friendly in their way too," said Debby. "It's just that a king has to strut and a queen has to mince."

When the sun began to go down behind the mountains, the birds went to roost in the trees, and Mother's chickens strolled into the hen house, one by one, to go to bed.

"Why don't the king and queen go to bed too?" Bonnie called to Mother in the kitchen.

Mother came to the door and watched the bantams strutting anxiously back and forth in a corner of the chicken yard. "They're not used to their new home yet," she said. "You and Debby had better catch them and put them inside. They'll go to bed by themselves after you once show them."

Debby and Bonnie hurried to the chicken yard. They called Chris to help them.

Together they cornered the bantams against the fence, caught them, put them on the roost inside the castle, and shut the door.

Debby and Bonnie waited until the king and queen had had time to settle down. Then they peeped inside. There, close together on the toy broomstick sat King Strut and Queen Mince, their toy toes curled firmly around the stick, their toy eyes tightly shut.

The next morning, which was Sunday, while Bonnie and Debby were washing and drying the breakfast dishes for Mother, they heard a toy to-do in the castle. Queen Mince was cackling gaily and King Strut was chuckling proud toy noises in his throat.

Debby and Bonnie hurried to the castle. There in the nest, which was no bigger than a saucer, Queen Mince had laid an egg which was no bigger than a toy egg. They took it out of the nest and ran to show it to Father and Mother.

"Maybe she'll lay a lot of eggs," said Debby.

132

"And we'll set them and have a whole flock of little bantam princes and princesses," said Bonnie.

"Better not set bantam eggs till spring," advised Father. "Bantams are so little they need lots of summer weather to grow in. Pretty soon it will be fall, the leaves will be turning, cold winds will be blow-

133

ing, and frost will kill the pumpkin vines. That kind of weather is hard on bantam princes and princesses."

"Will Queen Mince want to set in the spring?" asked Debby.

"Of course," said Father. "And even though she acts so proud, she will make the kindest, gentlest little mother on the whole farm."

"What shall we do with this egg?" asked Bonnie holding the warm, pinkish-brown toy egg in the palm of her hand.

"Whatever you like," said Father. "It belongs to you."

"You may eat it for your dinner if you like," suggested Mother.

"Oh, no!" cried Bonnie. "I wouldn't like to eat it."

"I wouldn't either," said Debby.

"Why don't you put it in a basket," suggested Mother, "and decide later what to do with it?"

They found a toy hickory basket that had belonged to Althy when she played with toys and laid the egg in it.

On Sunday afternoon after Bonnie and Debby had eaten their dinner, they went outside to play for the last time before starting to school on Monday.

First they romped with Dirtyknees. They pranced through the tall grass with the lamb at their heels. Sometimes they scampered into an apple tree. Then he stood underneath the tree and begged them to come down and play with him. "Baa-aa!" he begged. "Baa-aa-aa-aa!"

Bonnie tied a bright red ribbon on the back of his white woolly neck.

"Oh, Dirtyknees!" she sighed. "Mary's lamb never looked like you! Now let's see if you can follow me without butting. Easy, now, Dirtyknees!"

Through the grass they walked, Bonnie in front, Dirtyknees following behind, using his very best manners.

"Oh, I do hope Miss Cora will let him come to school!" said Debby.

After a while Hans came waddling down the hill through the tall grass. He was on his way to the stream to swim. Bonnie and Debby went with him.

135

Up and down the stream swam Hans, looking like a little yellow boat. While he swam, Debby and Bonnie waded in the cool water. They built dams of sand and gravel. They watched crayfishes scuttling backward among the pebbles. Once Debby caught a minnow in her hands.

When Hans had swum long enough, he climbed up on the bank and sunned himself. Then he waddled up the hill toward the chicken yard. Debby and Bonnie went too. On the way Bonnie caught a butterfly. Debby found an arrowhead.

At the castle they stopped to watch King Strut and Queen Mince. They looked inside the nest, but found no more eggs. Queen Mince had done her work for that day.

At last they went into the kitchen, sat down under the stairs where the light was dim, and looked at Jemima's kittens until it was time to set the supper table for Mother.

"You must go to bed early tonight," said Mother. "School begins tomorrow, you know."

The next morning, Bonnie and Debby, wearing their new dresses, and with their books under their arms, started down the road ahead of Althy, Chris and Emmy.

Dirtyknees stood watching them from the orchard.

"Baa-aa-aa!" he called to them.

"Good-by, Dirtyknees," they called back. "Be a good lamb. We'll ask Miss Cora first thing if you may come to school on Friday."

Farther along they saw Hans waddling down the hill for his morning swim.

"Good-by, Hans!" they called. "Take care of yourself."

Farther still they heard a noise coming from the direction of the castle. They stopped to listen. Queen Mince was almost splitting her throat with her toy cackling.

"She's laid another egg!" said Bonnie. "That makes two. Whatever shall we do with them?"

Down the road they walked, past the crossroads

where the Sawyers were not yet waiting, past the big chestnut tree, and up the mountain path.

"We didn't get very rich this summer, did we Debby?" asked Bonnie.

"Well," said Debby thoughtfully, "we haven't any money."

"But we have Dirtyknees," said Bonnie. "And Hans. And Hatty One, Hatty Two, and Hatty Three. And King Strut and Queen Mince. I feel awfully rich."

"And our two plates," said Bonnie.

They stopped when they were halfway up the mountain path and looked back. They could see Mrs.

Sawyer standing in the kitchen door of her house down in the hollow.

"I can almost see that picture of the fruit in her dining room," said Debby.

"Every home has a picture now," said Bonnie.

Higher they climbed. When they were almost to the top, they stopped to rest.

Bonnie sat down on a stone and looked far down into the hollow.

"I'm trying to see Dirtyknees," she said. "But all I can see is Father going to the stable."

"Why don't we give him Hatty One, Hatty Two, and Hatty Three?" asked Bonnie. "We could give them to him to catch mice, and they would still be ours."

"We'll tell him tonight," said Debby.

When they reached the highest point of the path, they stopped and looked back again.

"Look!" cried Bonnie. "Don't I see Old Mrs. Whitaker's wash on the line?"

As they looked toward the far end of the farthest hollow, something white fluttered in the wind.

"It is her wash," said Bonnie. "And it's white as snow."

"It's the sensational bluing," said Debby.

They stood a minute longer before turning to go down the mountain and across the footbridge to the schoolhouse.

"I know what we can do with the eggs, Debby," said Bonnie suddenly. "We can take them to Old Mr. and Mrs. Whitaker for a present."

"Maybe we can take them Saturday," said Debby. "Maybe Mother will let us spend the night."

"And maybe Old Mr. Whitaker will tell us that story about the Indian who saved him," said Bonnie.

"And the story about Solomon," said Debby.

"Maybe he'll play his fiddle for us too," said Bonnie. "Remember, Old Mrs. Whitaker said he might."

They started down the mountain. Soon they would come to the footbridge. Across the footbridge and through the woods was the schoolhouse. Miss Cora, the teacher, would be waiting for them.

"I feel richer than almost anybody in the world," said Bonnie.

143

About the Author

Rebecca Caudill is the pen name of Mrs. James S. Ayars. Born in 1899, she writes about herself: "One of eleven children, I was born on a rocky farm squeezed between the Black Mountains and the Poor Fork River in Harlan County, Kentucky" (*More About Junior Authors*). A few years later the family moved to Tennessee. While she attended highschool, young Miss Caudill "heard of college and decided to go to one. Having nary a penny to go on didn't strike me as an obstacle at all." She learned stenography, aided by an older sister, and with this skill, Miss Caudill was able to work her way through Wesleyan College in Macon, Georgia, "the first Wesleyan student ever to work for her education." After receiving a master's degree from Vanderbilt University, she proceeded to "see the world," doing teaching, office work and editing in such varied places as Rio de Janeiro, Toronto, and Nashville, Tennessee; and traveling throughout Europe. In these early days, she met another editor, James S. Ayars. They married and were to have two children. They lived in Urbana, Illinois, for many years.

Throughout their long married life, Rebecca, now Mrs. Ayars, and her husband encouraged one another in their respective writing talents. "My writing for children," she comments, "—even the re-writing—has been an exercise in joy. Most of my books are based on experiences of my own childhood spent in Appalachian Kentucky, and so are written from the heart," (*Twentieth Century Children's Authors*).

Mrs. Ayars' books for older children involve pioneer families in well-researched 18th and 19th century settings, often with a touch of mountain dialect. *The Far-off Land*, for instance, takes 16-year-old Ketty, with her brother, on a flatboat down the Holston and Tennessee Rivers. This book was inspired by an actual journal of 1779-1780, written by a colonel making such a flatboat voyage. In novels like this, with well-developed plots, Mrs. Ayars portrays the youthful heroine coming to terms with her own freedom to be a person in her own right and in obedience to her conscience.

Her books for younger children enlarge upon every-day pleasures and difficulties with a sense of wonder and freshness. *Schoolhouse in the Woods*, with *Happy Little Family* and the two novels that trace the same family's life in succeeding years are fine representatives of the author's appeal to young readers. She has also written with charm for the youngest children in books like *A Pocket Full of Cricket* and *A Certain Small Shepherd*—this last being a Christmas story, illustrated by William Pene du Bois. Mrs. Ayars died in 1985.

More Stories about the Fairchilds

Happy Little Family

We are introduced to the Fairchild family through the eyes of its youngest member, Bonnie, just four years old. Bonnie is more than ready to join her three older sisters and one brother in their many adventures—sliding on the ice, searching for arrowheads, proving their bravery and wisdom to Father, or going on that journey of all journeys, across the swinging bridge to school. Winter or summer, joys and sorrows alternate rapidly as Bonnie makes a point of keeping up with Debby, Emmy, Chris and Althy. Meanwhile Mother and Father provide all the security needed for growth and happiness in their home tucked amidst the pine trees of the Kentucky hills, one hundred years or more ago.

Schoolhouse in the Woods

Bonnie is waiting for her first day at school, waiting as only Bonnie can—with whole-hearted perseverance. Once again, Rebecca Caudill captures a glimpse of what life is like for the youngest child in any family, richly flavored, in this case, by the well-wrought atmosphere of Kentucky mountain life in the early 1900's. The reader experiences, with Bonnie, both the pain and pleasure of waiting for her father's return with her new first reader and slate, of her excruciating anticipation to wear her new school dresses. Monday finally arrives and Bonnie, for the first time, joins her brother and three sisters as they hurry down the river road, joining friends along the way. Once across the cable footbridge (without once holding on), she enters at last the little schoolhouse in the woods and its enchanting and beckoning world of new experiences. Bonnie's first school year fulfills all her hopes and more, except that for her, it is over far too soon. Well, she is getting practiced at waiting. No one can do *that* quite as well as she.

Schoolroom in the Parlor

School in the Kentucky hills goes from August to the last Friday before Christmas. After that the snows are too high, and later, the thawing rivers too full, for the Fairchild children, and their neighbors, the Wattersons, the Sawyers, and the Huffs to make it safely to the little schoolhouse in the woods. Now that Althy is fourteen, Mr. Fairchild has other plans for the long winter months. Learn, along with Bonnie, Debby, Chris and Emmy, what it is like to have school at home in the early 1900's. When spring comes, bringing with it an unexpected visitor, Bonnie discovers that she knows what it is she wants to do when she is grown-up—and she can hardly wait!